BREAD AND HONEY

• A FRANK ASCH BEAR BOOK •

BREAD AND HONEY

• FRANK ASCH •

ALADDIN

New York London Toronto Sydney New Delhi

ALADDIN

An imprint of Simon & Schuster Children's Publishing Division

1230 Avenue of the Americas, New York, NY 10020

This Aladdin edition March 2015

For information about special discounts for bulk purchases,

please contact Simon & Schuster Special Sales at 1-866-506-1949

or business@simonandschuster.com.

The Simon & Schuster Speakers Bureau can bring authors to your live event.

For more information or to book an event contact the

Simon & Schuster Speakers Bureau at 1-866-248-3049

or visit our website at www.simonspeakers.com.

Designed by Karina Granda

The text of this book was set in Olympian LT Std.

Manufactured in China 1214 SCP

2 4 6 8 10 9 7 5 3 1

Library of Congress Control Number 81-16893

ISBN 978-1-4424-6665-4 (hc)

ISBN 978-1-4424-6666-1 (pbk)

ISBN 978-1-4424-6667-8 (eBook)

To Tracy,
Shannon,
and Tina

One morning when Ben was getting
ready for school, his mother took a
loaf of fresh bread out of the oven.
"Can I have a piece?" asked Ben.

"The bread is too hot now," said his mother. "But you can have some when you get home."

"With honey on top?" asked Ben.

"Yes," said his mother, "with lots of honey on top."

"Okay," said Ben, and he hurried off to school.

That day, Ben painted
a picture of his mother.

When the bell rang, he
decided to take it home.

On the way, he stopped to show
the picture to Owl.

"I love it," said Owl. "But you
made the eyes too small."

"I have my paint box with me,"
said Ben. "Maybe I can fix that."

"Fine work!" said Owl.

At the riverbank, Ben showed the picture to Alligator.

"I just love it!" said Alligator. "But the mouth needs to be much, much bigger!"

"How's that?" asked Ben.
"Much better!" said Alligator.

A little way down the path, Ben met
Rabbit and showed her the picture.

"I love it!" said Rabbit. "But the
ears are too short."

"Oh, that's easy to fix," said Ben.

"How's that?" asked Ben.
"Wonderful," said Rabbit.

When Ben showed Elephant his
picture, Elephant said, "I love
it, but the nose is too small."

Once again, Ben took out his
paints.

"How's that?" asked Ben.

"Unforgettable!" said Elephant.

Then Ben showed his picture to Lion.

"I love it," said Lion. "But you
forgot a fluffy mane."

"How's that?" asked Ben.

"A picture to be proud of," said Lion.

When Ben was almost home,
he saw Giraffe and showed
him his picture.

"I just love it," said Giraffe.
"But the neck is too short."

"How's that?" asked Ben.

"Perfect," said Giraffe.

Ben ran the rest of the way home.
When he got there, he said to
his mother, "Look what I made—a
picture of you!"

"I love it!" said his mother.

"Just the way it is?" asked Ben.

"Just the way it is," said his mother.
And she hung it on the refrigerator.

Then she gave Ben a thick slice
of homemade bread with lots of
honey on top.